YOU CAN FLY

YOU CAN FLY

The Tuskegee Airmen

Carole Boston Weatherford

illustrated by **Jeffery Boston Weatherford**

ATHENEUM BOOKS FOR YOUNG READERS
New York London Toronto Sydney New Delhi

ATHENEUM BOOKS FOR YOUNG READERS
An imprint of Simon & Schuster Children's Publishing Division
1230 Avenue of the Americas, New York, New York 10020

ATHENEUM BOOKS FOR YOUNG READERS is a registered trademark of Simon & Schuster, Inc. Atheneum logo is a trademark of Simon & Schuster, Inc.
For information about special discounts for bulk purchases, please contact Simon & Schuster Special Sales at 1-866-506-1949 or business@simonandschuster.com.
The Simon & Schuster Speakers Bureau can bring authors to your live event. For more information or to book an event, contact the Simon & Schuster Speakers Bureau at 1-866-248-3049 or visit our website at www.simonspeakers.com.
The text for this book is set in Archer.
The illustrations for this book are rendered in scratchboard.
Manufactured in the United States of America
0416 FFG
First Edition
10 9 8 7 6 5 4 3 2 1
Library of Congress Cataloging-in-Publication Data
Weatherford, Carole Boston, 1956–
You can fly : the Tuskegee Airmen / Carole Boston Weatherford ; art by Jeffery Boston Weatherford.
pages cm
Includes bibliographical references.
Audience: Grades 4–6.
ISBN 978-1-4814-4938-0 (hardcover)
ISBN 978-1-4814-4940-3 (eBook)
1. World War, 1939–1945—Participation, African American—Juvenile poetry. 2. United States. Army Air Forces. Fighter Squadron, 99th—History—Juvenile poetry. 3. African American air pilots—History—Juvenile poetry. 4. World War, 1939–1945—Aerial operations, American—Juvenile poetry. 5. Tuskegee Army Air Field (Ala.)—Juvenile poetry. 6. World War, 1939–1945—Campaigns—Western Front—Juvenile poetry. I. Weatherford, Jeffery Boston, artist. II. Title.
PS3623.E375Y68 2015
811'.6—dc23
2015012393

In memory of my father, Joseph A. Boston Jr.,
a World War II veteran.
To all who fly in their dreams
—C. B. W.

To my mom, my dad, and my tribe
—J. B. W.

CONTENTS

YOU CAN FLY

Head to the Sky

No matter that there are only 130
licensed black pilots in the whole nation.
Your goal of being a pilot cannot be grounded
by top brass claiming blacks are not fit to fly.
Your vision of planes cannot be
blocked by clouds of doubt.
The engine of your ambition will not brake
for walls of injustice—no matter how high.

The sky's no limit if you've flown
on your own power in countless dreams;
not if you've raised homing pigeons
on Harlem rooftops;
or watched crop dusters
buzzing over rows of cotton;
not if you've gazed at stars
and known God meant for you to soar.

The Civilian Pilot Training Program

You see the posters: Uncle Sam Wants You.
If only that meant in the cockpit.
But the Civilian Pilot Training Program—
the CPTP—is for whites only
until the NAACP and black newspapers push
Congress to fund programs at several black colleges—
including Howard, Hampton, and Tuskegee—
and at the Coffey School of Aeronautics.
Of more than 400,000 pilots trained
by the CPTP, only 2,000 are black;
less than half of a percent.
Yet 2,000 dreams of flight
are finally off the ground.

Train Ride to the Clouds

All aboard for Tuskegee Institute,
where Booker T. Washington uplifted ex-slaves
and George Washington Carver
is working wonders with sweet potatoes!

If Carver can make paint
from clay and plastics from soy,
then the school Booker T. founded
can surely make you a pilot.

If you did not believe that were true
you would not have packed your bag
and boarded the train for Alabama
with a Bible and a box lunch from your mama.

If your faith were not vast as the sky,
you would never have taken this leap.

A Shot

At Tuskegee, you answer to "Chief" Anderson.
He's flown coast to coast and is up to training
black civilian pilots over red clay hills.
But can he win over the First Lady?

When Eleanor Roosevelt visits,
Chief takes her on a short hop in his plane—
despite warnings to the contrary.
Mrs. Roosevelt hangs on to her hat!

No question in her mind now
about blacks in the cockpit.
You can fly, she says.
Back at the White House,
the First Lady sways the president.
He orders the army to give black pilots a shot.

The code-named Tuskegee Experiment begins.
Moton Field and an airfield complex
costing more than a million dollars
go up in six short months.

Not one minute too soon.
Your head has been in the clouds for years.

The First Cadets

You hail from big cities and country roads
and are not run of the mill by any measure.
Thirteen men—not thirty-five, as expected—
and not an "average Joe" among you.
Several college grads, a policeman,
a factory inspector, a scholar-athlete,
two trained civilian pilots,
and at least one who hounded

the Army Air Corps for a slot.
He was the first to be contacted.
The most distinguished?
Lieutenant Colonel Benjamin O. Davis Jr.,
whose father is a first lieutenant,
graduated West Point—in 1936,
the first black graduate of the twentieth century—
even though his classmates shunned him.
As a boy, Davis idolized Charles Lindbergh—
the first pilot to cross the Atlantic alone, nonstop—
and had his first flight when his father
paid a barnstormer five dollars for a ride.

Officers

You are in Class 42-C under all-white command.
Your first lesson: to "Yes, sir!"
and "Sir, no sir!" your officers.

Major James A. Ellison, a pull-no-punches
straight shooter who aims to fly cross country
with his all-black squadron, just to show it can be done.

Lt. Colonel Noel Parrish,
who doesn't have a racist bone
in his body and tires of questions
about your qualifications to fly.

Captain Gabe Hawkins, Captain Robert Long,
and Major Donald McPherson—
who all have as much to prove as you.

For them, choosing Tuskegee
means never making general,
but making history instead.

Yes, sir!

The Odds

As you stand at attention, your commander
tells you cadets to look left and right.
The men beside you may not make it.
You glance at your comrades,
hoping you all beat the odds.
You pray every night to make the cut.

Your God-fearing mama writes
that folks back home are on their knees
sending up timber for you—
their favorite son.
You vow not to wash out.

Tuskegee is a laboratory,
and you are under a microscope.
But the distance to your goal
is longer than any airstrip.

The burden of past and future,
heavier than any aircraft.
The eyes of your country are on you;

the hopes of your people
rest on your shoulders.

Some days, you look heavenward—
sensing that it might be easier
to defy gravity than Jim Crow.

Keep 'Em Flying: Tuskegee Army Airfield Nurses

You cannot go to war without a medical corps.
A shortage of nurses finally forces the military
to let black women into the Army Nurse Corps.

Of 50,000 nurses serving, maybe 500 are black.
The twenty-nine at Tuskegee Army Airfield
face discrimination because of race and gender.

But the nurses cannot cure the disease of prejudice.
All these second lieutenants can do is their duty.
There is nothing better than a good nurse.

As medical, surgical, and dispensary nurses,
the women man the station hospital
and work the wards day and night.

Nursing school grads, registered nurses, all
under principal chief nurse Della "Maw" Raney—
the first black woman in the Army Nurse Corps.
First lieutenant to you.

Your buddy, Airman Chuck Dryden,
marries Irma Cameron, a nurse from Harlem
who goes by "Pete."
Three nurses you know ship out to Liberia.

It really takes a good nurse to KEEP 'EM FLYING.

Ground School

In the classroom, you study math,
       map reading, science and engineering,
             learn what makes planes fly,
        how weather affects flight,
    and to communicate in code.
Enough to make your head spin.

Walking back to the barracks one day
       with your notebook under your arm,
           you see geese gliding in V-formation
              through a cloudless sky.
         You can't help but think:
    One day that will be me.

And, sure enough, thanks to your brother pilots,
       you are more than ready for the test.
           You spend hours in wooden chairs
              cramming aeronautics into
          your earthbound brains.
    The plane's body is steel, its blood, fuel;
but you will be its brain.

The midnight oil pays off. You pass the test
         to join the ranks that couldn't be
                  kept down: future aircraft mechanics,
                           control tower operators,
                  armament specialists, radio repairmen,
         police, parachute riggers, and, yes,
pilots training at Tuskegee.

You are walking on air and sprouting wings.

Solo, At Last

You are shaking in your boots
when you climb into that PT-17.
You watch your instructor
work the plane's controls.
Then you use the stick to change speed,
altitude, and direction.

You move the control column
and foot pedals to maneuver
the wings and tail. You do takeoffs
and landings, mimicking your instructor's
every move. And you watch fellow cadets,
one by one, fly solo.

Guys who never saw a plane up close
before arriving at Tuskegee
do loops and barrel rolls in midair.
You tease cadets who get airsick
and throw up over the side.
That's known as feeding the buzzards.

Finally, your moment.
After eight hours of lessons,
it's your turn to fly solo,
to conquer a new world.
You steer as if you and the plane are one.
You have never felt freer.
Never.

Sugar, Sugar

You love Hershey's bars,
but letters from home are sweeter.
Hearing your name during mail call
is like being lifted by a prayer.

When you get mail from your girl,
you rip open the envelope,
read the letter at least three times,
and stash it in your footlocker.

You pin her picture on the wall
beside your bunk. Every night,
hers is the last face you see.
You aim to marry her after the war.

The Other War

While your squadron trains,
awaits combat orders,
bigots wage a different war
on dark roads and town squares.

In this war, the enemy is you.
In 1941 and 1942, eleven black men—
if you count the three boys—
were lynched in the United States.

Army-trained, but defenseless
against the prejudice you face at every turn,
you don't stray far from base.

Downtime

Ain't much to do in tiny Tuskegee,
And most night spots
in neighboring towns don't allow blacks.
You try not to go stir crazy.
To unwind, you play cards—
pinochle, poker, or spades.
On a good night, you win.

In the theater on base, all-black movies fill the bill:
Herbert Jeffries in *The Bronze Buckaroo*,
Paul Robeson in *Song of Freedom*,
The Heavenly Choir in *The Blood of Jesus*,
and Lena Horne in *The Duke Is Tops*.
When sepia stars light the screen
who needs wings to fly?

Training Planes

You still fly
in your dreams
but no longer
with your own wings.
Now you pilot training planes,
practicing even in your sleep.

You do landings, spins, loops,
and vertical climbs,
and fly upside down
in the BT-13 Valiant.
It has a two-way radio
and one heckuva engine.

You fly in formation in the AT-6.
She has a full-metal fuselage,
a machine-gun mount,
and a 650-horsepower engine.
Cruising at 160 miles an hour,
your reflexes have got to be fast.

In the P-40, a single-seat, single-engine
armored shark, you fly low
for a ground attack.
That Warhawk can outgun
swifter, nimbler planes;
can take a hit and have firepower to spare.

You have a dogfight on your hands.
Budda budda budda budda!
Budda budda budda budda!

Beyond the horizon, a bugle plays reveille.
You wake from your dream.
Time to don your flight gear.

Pearl Harbor

You are in the mess hall,
when the news hits you like a tank.
Japanese bombs rained
on Pearl Harbor's Battleship Row,
pummeling vessels in port:
the *Maryland, Tennessee, California,*
Utah, Nevada, Oklahoma,
West Virginia, and *Arizona,*

and the drydocked *Pennsylvania*.
Three battleships sank.

What bombs didn't smash,
torpedos slammed.
The losses all told:
eighteen ships hit
and nearly three hundred aircraft destroyed or damaged.

In two short hours,
the Pacific Fleet—destroyed,
and 2,403 Americans—dead.
Smoke clouds turned day to dark,
and united a nation in prayer.

December 7, 1941—
a date that President Roosevelt says
will live in infamy.
The United States declares war on Japan.
You cannot wait to earn your stripes.

Dorie Miller Earns the Navy Cross

You hear that Dorie grew up wrestling
his three brothers and playing fullback
on the high school football team
before serving as a cook in the navy
and becoming his ship's heavyweight boxing champ.

His name is in the news of the attack on Pearl Harbor.
He was collecting laundry on the USS *West Virginia*
when the alarm sounded. He rushed toward
his battle station and found it
wrecked by torpedo damage.

On deck, he was given orders.
Carry wounded sailors to safer places;
then go to the bridge.
Help the mortally wounded captain.
Dorie followed the orders.

Although untrained on the weapon,
Dorie then manned a .50-caliber
antiaircraft machine gun
until the ammunition was gone
and he was ordered to abandon ship.

It wasn't hard, he said.
I just pulled the trigger and she worked fine.
I had watched the others with these guns.
I guess I fired her for about fifteen minutes.
I think I got one of those Jap planes.
They were diving pretty close to us.

The USS *West Virginia* had been hit by two bombs
through her deck and five torpedoes into her port side.
Of the more than fifteen hundred men on board,
130 were killed and 52 were wounded.

Dorie Miller was awarded the Navy Cross.
The Secretary of the Navy stated,
This marks the first time in this conflict
that such high tribute
has been made . . . to a member of his race. . . .
The future will see others similarly honored
for brave acts.

You bet it will, you say. *You bet.*

Private Joe Louis

You have cheered for boxer Joe Louis
since he won the Golden Gloves as an amateur.
Known as the Brown Bomber,
Joe possessed a powerful left jab
and pounding two-fisted attack.
He was the first black hero
that all America worshipped.

Joe won twelve contests the year he turned pro.
He climbed the heavyweight class
and soon was at the top of the boxing world,
save one loss to Max Schmeling.
He defeated Primo Carnera before a crowd
of thousands at Yankee Stadium.
Next, he knocked out Max Baer in the fourth round.
But Joe still hungered for revenge—
a second shot at Schmeling—and told fans
not to call him champ until he beat the German.

In 1938, Joe got his chance.
Americans leaned toward radios, rooting for Joe to win,
to knock out Nazism and to hand Hitler an upset.
Two minutes and forty seconds into the rematch,
Joe settled the score with a knockout.

After the attack on Pearl Harbor, Joe lent his fists
to the war effort. His benefit matches netted
nearly $125,000 for the army and navy relief funds.
He persuaded the War Department
to admit his friend and fellow athlete Jackie Robinson

into Officer Candidate School,
along with thirteen other men
whom racist policies had barred.
And he overcame a case of nerves to speak
at a Navy Relief Show at Madison Square Garden.
A man of few words, Joe delivered a knockout punch:
I'm real happy that I'm able enough. . . .
I'm only doing what any red-blooded American would.
We're gonna do our part
and we'll win 'cause we're on God's side.

Three days after the star-studded fund-raiser,
Joe enlisted, turning down an officer's commission
to be an ordinary G.I.
But Louis was no ordinary soldier or "ordinary Joe."
Before long, he appeared in uniform
on a recruiting poster.
The army even quoted his speech.

You gotta respect a guy like Joe.

Fighting Boredom

You long for action, but days drag on.
America's fists are aimed at two fronts,
yet you've got time on your hands.
Even practice maneuvers get humdrum.

Then someone devises a stunt.
The pilot flies under two bridges
and a low-hanging power line,
and into a loop. Over and over,
you take turns doing that trick—
until Lawson and Dawson
go down, leaving Dawson dead.

That could have been you.

Second Lieutenant

Hard to tell whose chests
stick out more
on graduation day—
yours or your white officers'.

At the ceremony,
your mother wears
her Sunday best and pins
hard-earned silver wings
on your dress uniform.

You have never stood so tall
or seen her smile as long.
Second lieutenant.

William Henry Hastie

A Phi Beta Kappa, first-in-class graduate
of Amherst College, William Henry Hastie
is the man to have your corner.
He followed the path cleared by his mentor,
legal lion Charles Hamilton Houston—
from college to Harvard Law, into private practice,
then teaching and a deanship
at all-black Howard Law School
and finally into the battle to topple Jim Crow.

When named civilian aide to Secretary of War
Henry Stimson, Hastie had already argued
an NAACP lawsuit and served as a judge—
the first African American on the federal bench.
He is nobody's rubber stamp.
Like you, he is a freedom fighter.

Touring military posts, Hastie sees separate
and unequal armies, one black and one white.
One robbed of a fair chance,
the other realizing rank and promise.

Despite Hastie's findings, Stimson backs the policy:
Blacks are not meant to take charge.

Hastie bristles at such notions.
With the military in lockstep, he presses
to get black troops their due, for he knows
that you bleed the same as whites.

How could a black man be expected to fight,
he asks, *and defend a country*
that doesn't respect his rights . . . ?

The Double V Campaign: Pens Mighty as Swords

For news of your people, you look to the black press.
You subscribe to *The Pittsburgh Courier*,
the largest black newspaper in the nation.
If the *Courier* gives voice to black America,
then James G. Thompson, a reader from Kansas,
echoes the paradox faced by every black enlisted man.
In 1942, Thompson writes a letter to the newspaper
asking, *Should I sacrifice to live half American?*

Draft age, he wonders if equality is too much
to demand in exchange for military service;
if a segregated America is worth defending;
if color barriers will topple after the war;
if the next generation will have better opportunities.

Thompson claims racism is destroying democracy
just as surely as fascist dictators
Hitler, Mussolini, and Franco.
Stressing a willingness to die for his country,
Thompson advocates a Double V campaign

for victory on the battlefield and the homefront.
He calls on blacks to support the war
on foreign soil and to push for justice at home.

Moved to act, the *Courier* launches a campaign—
Democracy, At Home, Abroad—
complete with a Double V logo for double victories.
The paper's 200,000 readers rally for the cause.
Letters, telegrams pour in from across the nation.
There are Double V baseball games, gardens,
beauty pageants, dresses, hats, dances, and bands.
The *Courier* runs daily photos of Double V girls.

Double V clubs assemble care packages
for troops overseas, sell war bonds,
meet with businessmen about employment
    discrimination,
and write Congress to protest poll taxes
that effectively deny black citizens the vote.
Other newspapers soon join the fight.

For one year at the beginning of World War II,
Thompson's pen is a sword.
FBI Director J. Edgar Hoover deems Double V
an act of treason.
But for you, it is a call to conscience,
a blow to Jim Crow.

Anxious

You are itching to fight.
How can America win, you wonder,
with one arm tied? With black troops
stuck as second-class soldiers,
barred from the skirmishes
in the skies?

First Lady Eleanor Roosevelt asks: *Why?*
Secretary of War Henry Stimson,
who never liked the notion of black pilots,
comes to see for himself.
You show what you can do;
he declares you outstanding by any standard.

Then the order comes,
the words you have waited
a year to hear: Move out!
Four hundred of you
from the 99th Fighter Squadron
board a train for New York.

Jim Crow follows you
from Alabama on to the Atlantic.
On the SS *Mariposa*—
a luxury liner turned troop ship—
a rope separates black soldiers from white.
You are almost flying too high to care.

The Fight Song

Contact—
Joy stick back—
Sailing through the blue
Gallant sons of the 99th—
Brown men tried and true

We are the Heroes of the night—
To hell with the Axis might
FIGHT! FIGHT! FIGHT! FIGHT!
Fighting 99th.

Rat-tat, Rat-tat-tat—
Down in flames they go
The withering fire of the 99th—
Sends them down below

We are the Heroes of the night—
To hell with the Axis might
FIGHT! FIGHT! FIGHT! FIGHT!
Fighting 99th.

Drink up, Drain your cup—
To those daring men
Flying torch of flame, Oh GOD—
Red White and Blue—Amen.

For We Are—

Heroes of the night
To hell with the Axis might
FIGHT! FIGHT! FIGHT! FIGHT!
Fighting 99th WINGS!!

Facing the Enemy

Even though seven of your guys fight off
the enemy in aerial combat,
and Charlie Hall—on his eighth mission—
hits the first enemy plane
downed by a Tuskegee Airman,
the top brass still cook up
obstacles to ground you.
Fighter pilots are even ordered
to lose their black escorts.
But you don't let them.

When Lieutenant Colonel Davis reaches
Washington, the War Department is humming
with reports that blacks lack brains and grit.
While you defend democracy abroad,
Davis must defend you at home.

He is convincing.
The committee orders another study.
If policymakers had had their way,
the Tuskegee Experiment would have ended.
For now, you and Davis have won.

Operation Prove Them Wrong

You are in Operation Corkscrew,
wingmen to fighter pilots of the all-white 33rd,
when, after ten days, air power alone
overcomes the nine-mile island of Pantelleria,
clearing the way to Sicily.
You are in the Battle of Anzio, patrolling
the skies as Allied ships unload.
Enemy gunners scream down but can't buy
a clear shot. You dodge flak and fire back.
In two days, you shoot down twelve German planes.

You are in Operation Diadem,
capturing the ruin atop Monte Cassino
and a Distinguished Unit Citation as well,
the second for the Tuskegee Airmen.
But nothing beats shelling a destroyer
with bullets alone. You do that
off the Adriatic Coast—without one bomb,
with only machine-gun fire and aim
sure enough to pelt a ship and hit its weapons cache.
A blaze, a smoke cloud, then a blast.

Missions last five hours, sometimes six.
The longer the flight, the hotter
the cockpit seems. In the sun,
you sweat through a flight jacket
before one shot is fired.
Peering through a Plexiglas window—
the only thing between you and the Nazis—
you can't help but pity them.
They have no clue what you are made of—
that you cut your teeth battling the color barrier,
that you've seen enough action for two wars.

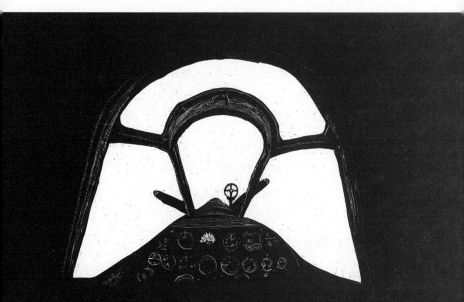

Routines

Motto of the Tuskegee Airmen's ground crews:
Do it right the first time.

Every time you climb into the cockpit,
you ask God to be your copilot.
Not long ago, flying army planes
was a dream reserved for white men.
You think of your family back home.
If only they could see you.

Every time you push the throttle,
you thank the crews who work
amid deafening noise, spinning propellers,
and the constant threat of an airfield attack.
Up at 5 a.m. readying planes, crews leap
into action again the second planes land.

Every time you take off,
you thank the crewmen who check the wings
and landing gear, patch battle scars,
and tune up and refuel the engines.
For every hour a plane is in the air,
crews work ten on the ground to keep 'em flying.

Every time you win a dogfight,
you thank the armament specialists who remove
the plane's .50-caliber machine guns, clean them,
put them back in place, and load them
with white-tipped phosphorous bullets.

Every time your plane lands,
you thank Lieutenant Colonel Benjamin Davis Jr.
He knows you have one shot, no second chances,
and he refuses to let you fail.
He pushes you to fly higher
so that nothing can hold you down.

Lena Horne: More than a Pin-Up

A wartime pinup is worth a thousand kisses.
Hollywood hands out thousands of glamour photos:
redheaded goddess Rita Hayworth,
buxom Jane Russell leaning against a haystack,
Dorothy Lamour wrapped in a sarong,
"The Sweater Girl" Lana Turner,
Betty Grable in a bathing suit
baring her million-dollar legs.
The top brass figure these pinups raise morale.

There is but one star you black troops call your own.
On stage since age sixteen, Lena Horne
started on Cotton Club's chorus line,
hoofing to Duke and Cab's big bands.
From there to Broadway and then Hollywood;
the first black actress signed to a studio contract.
But Lena will not play a maid,
so her roles are few;
mostly singing numbers that can be easily cut
for Southern theaters that refuse

to screen her black beauty.
Lena dubs herself "a butterfly pinned to a column."
Still, she soars in black films like *Cabin in the Sky*
and *Stormy Weather*, whose title song
is her signature.

This songbird does her part for the war effort,
posing in an apron for a campaign to conserve energy.
And she performs live on USO tours
until black soldiers are barred
from one of her concerts
and seated behind German prisoners at another.
Lena knows racism well. She has headlined venues
where she isn't allowed to sleep or eat. Fed up,
she stops working at whites-only establishments
and quits the USO tours, too.

Now Lena pays her own way
to perform for troops. When she visits Tuskegee,
she sings, perches in planes, and poses for photos.
How could you not fall for Lena?

Red Tail Angels

With .50-caliber machine guns and a 500-pound
bomb load, the tublike P-47 is built for combat.
You dub it "the Jug." Your ground crew
paints the plane's tail and propellers a jazzy red.

You fly those planes deep into enemy territory.
But the Germans plan to strike
the bombers close to base
before any black escorts can shield them.

On a hunch you trail the bombers
right from takeoff—like guardian angels.
Two dozen German 109s zoom in.
Davis yells, *Go get 'em!*

You face more than one hundred
German fighters. Yet you outgun them.
Five enemy planes explode,
one by one in midair.

That earns Lieutenant Colonel Davis
a Distinguished Flying Cross,
and you Tuskegee pilots a fitting nickname:
the Red Tail Angels.

The Black Birdmen

March 1945. You can almost smell victory.
Still, the Allies have no match
for the Nazi's speed demons: the Messerschmitt 163
and its sister the 262, Me's for short.
Topping five hundred miles per hour,
they are Germany's last shot at dragging out
a war it cannot win. The Allies bomb
German airplane factories, but hundreds
of Me's have already flown off assembly lines.

On an escort mission to Berlin,
the 332nd Fighter Group faces Me-262s
for the first time. They're fast, but German pilots
haven't quite gotten the hang of flying them yet,
giving you an edge. You hold your own;
do not lose one bomber. Not one.
A Distinguished Unit Citation attests to that.
But three of your pilots lose their lives.

The Germans call you Black Birdmen.
Schwarze Vogelmenshen.

You are racking up kills
in the European theater's last aerial battle
while Hitler is in his bunker
plotting suicide and planning his last meal.
Just before the Nazis surrender,
you fly your final mission.

By June 1945, you are home.

Your Record

The color barrier was granite,
but you not only chipped away at it,
you did victory rolls over the rubble.
And you glimpsed the other side.
The numbers speak louder than words.

In fifteen hundred combat missions, you blasted
one enemy destroyer, 262 German planes,
and 950 vehicles.
Of 205 missions, you flew 200
without losing one bomber—

a record that is yours alone.
You even boasted an ace pilot—
Lee Archer Jr., who shot down four enemy planes.

Of nearly a thousand Tuskegee pilots,
half went overseas
and fewer than a hundred were captured or killed.
For courage in combat: Distinguished Crosses,
Bronze Stars, and Purple Hearts—900–plus medals.
You conquered more than the skies.

No Hero's Welcome

No use candy-coating the truth:
Gasoline and sugar were rationed
during the war, and metal was reserved
for the defense industry,
but racism was never in short supply.
There was plenty of prejudice to go around
and you don't have to look far to find it
even after you get home.

You pass through South Carolina;
you see places that bar blacks
serving German prisoners of war.
You get wind of the Freeman Field Mutiny:
Pilots from the 477th Bombardment Group,
who never got to see combat before war's end,
got arrested in Indiana for storming
into the all-white officers' club.

Your fight is by no means finished.

A Long Line

You come from a long line of warriors.
You were Egyptian pharaohs giving rise
to civilization and pyramids along the Nile.
You were Hannibal atop an elephant
leading an army through the Alps and Pyrenees.
You were the Moors conquering Spain
and erecting great mosques in Granada and Córdoba.
You were Sonni Ali building the Timbuktu empire
and Shaka Zulu revolutionizing warfare
in Southern Africa.

Your perilous path was paved by patriots.
You were Crispus Attucks leading the charge
against the British in the Boston Massacre,
and becoming the first casualty
of the American Revolution.
You were Peter Salem, fatally shooting
the Redcoats' commander at the Battle of Bunker Hill.
You were Toussaint L'Ouverture, liberating slaves
and freeing Haiti from colonial rule.
You were Joseph Savary, single-handedly

raising a battalion to wage the Battle of New Orleans
in the War of 1812.

You hail from history-making heroes.
You were Martin R. Delany, becoming a field officer
after convincing Lincoln to let black men fight
and recruiting thousands for the U.S. Colored Troops.
You were Robert Smalls, sailing yourself to freedom
and then into history as the first
black navy captain in the Civil War.
You were Henry O. Flipper, who graduated West Point
despite the fact that he was never once spoken to
by a white cadet during his time at the military academy.
You were the Buffalo soldiers of the wild, wild West.

You descend from valiant soldiers.
You were the Harlem Hellfighters of World War I,
who never lost a man through capture,
never lost a trench, and never gave up
a foot of ground to the enemy.
You were the 5,000 black men who fought as Patriots,
the 200,000 in the U.S. Colored Troops,

and the 350,000 who served on the Western Front.
You fought in the Indian Wars
and the Spanish-American War.
You beat the drum and marched in victory parades.
When the fight was for freedom, you were there.

EPILOGUE

It is hereby declared to be the policy of the President that there shall be equality of treatment and opportunity for all persons in the armed services without regard to race, color, religion, or national origin.

—From Executive Order 9981, HARRY TRUMAN,
The White House, July 26, 1948

If you live long enough, you'll see
doors open and walls topple,
world powers rise and fall,
a King fight for justice
and a black general chairing
the Joint Chiefs of Staff.

You'll see Jackie Robinson
break baseball's color barrier
in a Brooklyn Dodgers uniform.
You'll remark, *It is high time.*

If you live long enough, you'll see
your share of shooting stars, an eclipse
or two, and perhaps Halley's Comet.
You'll see wounds heal and scars fade,
your sweetheart grow wise with you,
and your grandchildren graduate from college.

If you live long enough, you'll see
man land on the moon,
and black astronauts man spaceships.
You will see a new millennium dawn,
and hold a Congressional Gold Medal
in the palm of your hand.

You'll sit up front with lawmakers
when the first black president is sworn in.
And you will know your fight
was worth it.

AUTHOR'S NOTE

Although African-American soldiers have fought bravely throughout U.S. history, they were long denied skilled training and leadership roles in the armed forces. Many white military officers believed blacks were unfit for combat duty. Even after the Civil War, troops were segregated by race. And before 1940, African Americans could not become pilots in the U.S. military.

Civil rights groups and black journalists pressed for change. In 1941 the Army Air Corps launched the so-called Tuskegee Experiment to train African Americans to fly and maintain combat aircraft. Trained at Tuskegee Institute, a black college in Alabama, the graduates of the aviation training program became known as the Tuskegee Airmen. The military chose Tuskegee Institute because it had the facilities, qualified instructors, and a good climate for year-round flying. What began as a civilian pilot training program soon became the center of African-American aviation during World War II. Among the ranks of Tuskegee Airmen were pilots, navigators, bombardiers, maintenance and support staff, instructors, and other soldiers who kept the planes in the air. Under the command of Colonel Benjamin O. Davis Jr., the Tuskegee fighter groups—made up of the 99th, 100th, 301st, and 302nd fighter squadrons—flew successful missions over Sicily, the Mediterranean, and North Africa.

During World War II, Tuskegee Airmen participated in bombing missions, and a myth evolved that they never lost a bomber to enemy fighters. While this wasn't actually the case, it's true that the black escorts did not lose a bomber in 200 of their 205 missions. The pioneering Tuskegee Airmen overcame racism and became a respected fighter squadron. They proved that African Americans were fit for the Army Air Corps. And they paved the way for full integration of the U.S. military—a move ordered by President Harry Truman in 1948.

TIME LINE

1865

June 2: Civil War ends.

December 24: The Ku Klux Klan, a violent white supremacist group, is founded in Pulaski, Tennessee.

1896

May 18: The U.S. Supreme Court rules in the landmark Plessy v. Ferguson that racial segregation is constitutional.

1909

February 12: The National Association for the Advancement of Colored People (NAACP) is founded.

1915

November 14: Booker T. Washington dies. The educator and former slave founded Tuskegee Institute, a historically black college, in Alabama in 1881.

1917

April 2: United States enters World War I. More than 380,000 African Americans serve in the wartime army.

1919

June 28: World War I ends.

Summer: Race riots erupt in several cities in the North and South during what is known as Red Summer.

1925

November 10: The War College issues a report upholding segregation in the U.S. Armed Forces.

1939

The U.S. Army includes 3,640 African-American men.

June 27: Congress passes the Civilian Pilot Training Act.

1940

The NAACP launches a campaign to desegregate the U.S. armed forces.

September 16: Congress passes a Selective Service Act requiring the military to enlist blacks. On the same day, the War Department announces that the Civil Aeronautics Authority, along with the U.S. Army, will train African-American aviation personnel.

October: President Franklin D. Roosevelt's administration announces that Negroes will be trained as military pilots in the Army Air Corps. The War Department also promotes Benjamin O. Davis Sr. as the first black general in the U.S. Army and Judge William H. Hastie, the first black federal judge, as a civilian advisor to Secretary of War Henry L. Stimson.

October 25: Benjamin O. Davis Sr. becomes a brigadier general in the U.S. Army, the first African American in history to achieve that rank.

1941

Labor leader and civil rights activist A. Philip Randolph threatens a march in Washington, D.C., to protest discrimination in the military and the defense industry. The march is canceled after President Franklin Roosevelt issues an executive order banning federal discrimination.

The Army Nurse Corps begins accepting African-American nurses.

January 16: The War Department announces plans to train pilots for a "Negro pursuit squadron" at Tuskegee, Alabama.

March 22: The 99th Pursuit Squadron is activated at Chanute Field, Illinois, under the command of Captain Harold R. Maddux, a white officer, but composed of

African-American enlisted men. The squadron eventually moves to Maxwell Field, Alabama.

March: First Lady Eleanor Roosevelt takes a flight with Charles Alfred "Chief" Anderson, Tuskegee Institute's chief instructor pilot.

July 12: Construction begins on Tuskegee Army Airfield.

July 19: The first class of aviation cadets (42-C) enter Preflight Training at Tuskegee Institute.

July 23: The Air Corps establishes an Air Corps Advanced Flying School at Tuskegee.

December 7: The Japanese attack Pearl Harbor in Hawaii, drawing the United States into World War II. The need for combat pilots skyrockets. Aboard the USS *Arizona*, Dorie Miller, a navy messman with no weapons training, downs four Japanese fighter planes during the attack, earning him the Navy Cross.

1942

African-American women are eligible to join the new Women's Army Auxiliary Corps.
First Lieutenant Della Raney is selected as the first African-American chief nurse in the Army Nurse Corps while serving at Tuskegee Airfield, Alabama.

February 19: The 100th Pursuit Squadron is activated at Tuskegee Army Airfield, Alabama.

March 7: The first class of African-American pilots at Tuskegee Army Airfield complete advanced pilot training.

August 22: Lt. Col. Benjamin O. Davis Jr. becomes commander of the 99th Fighter Squadron.

1943

African-American women are eligible to join the new Women's Navy Corps.

William Henry Hastie, a former federal judge, resigns as aide to the U.S. Secretary of War to protest discrimination in the military.

April 16: The 99th Fighter Squadron sails aboard the steamship *Mariposa* from New York to North Africa.

June 2: The 99th Fighter Squadron flies its first combat mission as part of Operation Diadem, patrolling over the Mediterranean Sea.

June 9: The 99th Fighter Squadron faces enemy aircraft for the first time during an escort mission over Pantelleria Island, Italy, as part of Operation Corkscrew.

July 2: 1st Lt. Charles B. Hall of the 99th Fighter Squadron shoots down an enemy aircraft during a raid in Sicily, Italy—the first Tuskegee Airmen aerial victory credit. On the same day, 1st Lt. Sherman H. White and 2nd Lt. James L. McCullin are the first Tuskegee Airmen lost in combat. That afternoon, General Dwight D. Eisenhower visits the 99th Fighter Squadron.

June–July: The 99th Fighter Squadron earns the first of its three World War II Distinguished Unit Citations for missions over Italy.

July 21: The 99th Fighter Squadron flies thirteen missions in one day.

1944

The U.S. Navy lifts its ban on African Americans serving at sea. African Americans are also allowed in the Marine Corps and Coast Guard, and the military begins integrating training, mess, and recreational facilities.

January 27: Ten Tuskegee Airmen shoot down a total of ten enemy airplanes off St. Peter's Beach near Anzio, Italy.

January 28: Two Tuskegee Airmen shoot down a total of three enemy airplanes that threatened American ground forces at Anzio, Italy.

June 25: Tuskegee Airmen sink a German destroyer with machine-gun fire from their airplanes.

September 10: Four Tuskegee Airmen are awarded the Distinguished Flying Cross.

1945
April 5 and 6: At Freeman Field, Indiana, more than one hundred African-American officers are locked in the stockade for entering a whites-only officers' club in protest.

June: Colonel Benjamin O. Davis Jr. takes command of Godman Field in Kentucky, becoming the first African American to command an air force base.

August 6 and 9: The United States drops atomic bombs first on Hiroshima and then on Nagasaki, Japan, killing or wounding 200,000 people.

August 14: World War II ends with the surrender of Japan. During the war, more than one million African Americans served in the U.S. Armed Forces.

1947
April 11: Jackie Robinson signs a Major League Baseball contract with the Brooklyn Dodgers, becoming the league's first African-American player.

1948

President Harry Truman issues Executive Order 9981, ending segregation in the U.S. Armed Forces.

2007

March 29: Tuskegee Airmen are presented with the Congressional Medal of Honor at a ceremony at the U.S. Capitol.

2009

January 20: Tuskegee Airmen are invited guests at the inauguration of Barack Obama as the first African-American president of the United States.

RESOURCES

Further Reading

Homan, Lynn M., and Thomas Reilly. Illustrated by Rosalie M. Shepherd. *The Tuskegee Airmen Story*. Gretna, LA: Pelican Publishing Co., Inc., 2002.

Caver, Joseph, Jerome Ennels, and Daniel Haulman. *The Tuskegee Airmen: An Illustrated History: 1939–1949*. Montgomery, AL: NewSouth Books, 2011.

Hasday, Judy L. *The Tuskegee Airmen*. Philadelphia, PA: Chelsea House Publishers, 2003.

Stentiford, Barry M. *Tuskegee Airmen*. Santa Barbara, CA: Greenwood, 2011.

Moye, J. Todd. *Freedom Flyers: The Tuskegee Airmen of World War II*. New York: Oxford University Press, 2010.

Haulman, Daniel L. "Tuskegee Airmen Chronology." Air Force Historical Research Agency, 2010. www.afhso.af.mil/shared/media/document/AFD-101222-041.pdf

Museums and Online Resources

Tuskegee Airmen National Historic Site (Tuskegee, AL) www.nps.gov/tuai/index.htm

The Tuskegee Airmen National Historical Museum (Detroit, MI) tuskegeemuseum.org

National Museum of the U.S. Air Force (near Dayton, OH) www.nationalmuseum.af.mil/Visit/FactSheets/Display/tabid/509/Article/196131/tuskegee-airmen.aspx

The National WWII Museum (New Orleans, LA) www.nationalww2museum.org/see-hear/collections/focus-on/tuskegee-airmen.html

Tuskegee Airmen Inc. tuskegeeairmen.org

Tuskegee University/Tuskegee Airmen www.tuskegee.edu/about_us/legacy_of_fame/tuskegee_airmen.aspx

The Commemorative Air Force Red Tail Squadron www.redtail.org

Films

The Tuskegee Airmen (1995)
Red Tails (2012)

Primary Source Documents

While researching the Tuskegee Airmen, I found many
primary sources from the World War II era. These
documents and audiovisual materials helped me to interpret
history through poetry.

"Wings for This Man" is a World War II–era public service
newsreel about the Tuskegee Airmen. The 1945 film is
narrated by actor and future president Ronald Reagan.
View it here:
www.archive.org/details/gov.ntis.ava08663vnb1

The National Archives digital collection includes pictures
of African Americans in World War II, including some of
the Tuskegee Airmen. View them here:
www.archives.gov/research/african-americans/ww2-
pictures

The U.S. Army War College issued a memorandum in
1925 concluding that blacks were unfit for combat or
leadership and that black and white troops should remain
segregated. Read excerpts from "Memorandum for the

Chief of Staff regarding Employment of Negro Man Power in War, November 10, 1925" here:
herb.ashp.cuny.edu/items/show/808#document

In March 1941, during First Lady Eleanor Roosevelt's visit to Tuskegee Institute, flight instructor Charles Alfred "Chief" Anderson took her for a ride in a training plane. She described the flight in her newspaper column on April 1, 1941, and took home a photograph to show her husband, President Franklin D. Roosevelt, that black men could be pilots.
www.fdrlibrary.marist.edu/aboutfdr/tuskegee.html

On July 26, 1948, President Harry S. Truman issued Executive Order 9981, calling for equality of treatment and opportunity for all persons in the U.S. armed services. Read the document here:
www.trumanlibrary.org/9981.htm

The National WWII Museum's collection includes an oral history project. Several Tuskegee Airmen recall their military experiences in this video:
youtu.be/HCmceCQQW1Q

Carole Boston Weatherford is the acclaimed author of more than forty books, including *Voice of Freedom: Fannie Lou Hamer*, winner of a Caldecott Honor and a Sibert Honor; *Gordon Parks: How the Photographer Captured Black and White America*, winner of an NAACP Image Award; and *Moses: When Harriet Tubman Led Her People to Freedom*, winner of a Caldecott Honor, the Coretta Scott King Illustrator Award, and an NAACP Image Award. She is also the recipient of the North Carolina Award for Literature. Carole lives in North Carolina and teaches at Fayetteville State University. Visit her at CBWeatherford.com.

Jeffery Boston Weatherford created the scratch-board illustrations in this book using archival World War II photographs as reference. Jeffery studied art at Winston-Salem State University, where he was a Chancellor's Scholar, and at Howard University, where he earned a Master of Fine Arts.